CALL ME
FRANCIS TUCKET

OTHER YEARLING BOOKS BY GARY PAULSEN YOU WILL ENJOY:

YEARLING BOOKS are designed especially to entertain and enlighten young people. Patricia Reilly Giff, consultant to this series, received her bachelor's degree from Marymount College and a master's degree in history from St. John's University. She holds a Professional Diploma in Reading and a Doctorate of Humane Letters from Hofstra University. She was a teacher and reading consultant for many years, and is the author of numerous books for young readers.

CALL ME FRANCIS TUCKET

Gary Paulsen

A YEARLING BOOK

Published by
Dell Yearling
an imprint of
Random House Children's Books
a division of Random House, Inc.
1540 Broadway
New York, New York 10036

Visit us on the Web! www.randomhouse.com/kids

Educators and librarians, for a variety of teaching tools, visit us at www.randomhouse.com/teachers

ISBN: 0-440-41270-6

Reprinted by arrangement with Delacorte Press

Printed in the United States of America

November 1996

20   19   18   17   16   15

OPM

Dedicated to Jeff Edwards and Joe Fine for their devotion to excellence, and to Sequoyah, Cimarron, Summit, and Central middle schools and all their students and faculty

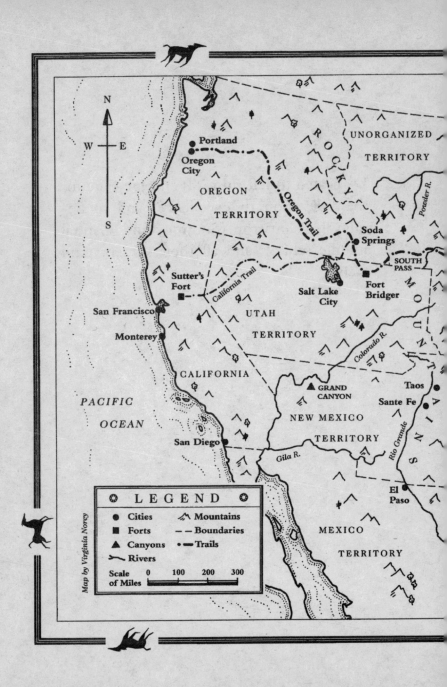

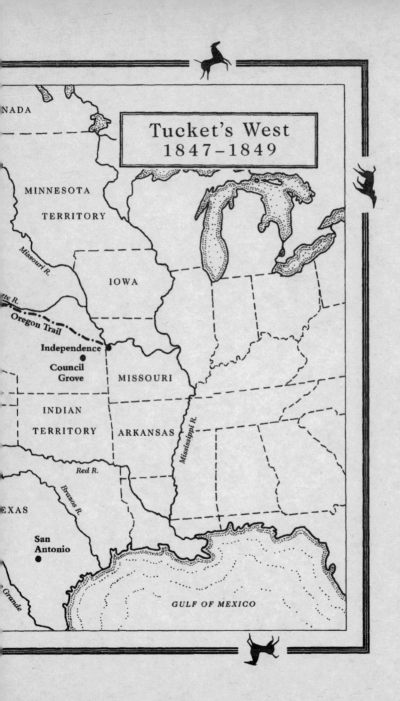

Tucket's West
1847–1849

NADA

MINNESOTA
TERRITORY

Missouri R.

IOWA

Platte R.

Oregon Trail

Independence

Council
Grove

MISSOURI

INDIAN

TERRITORY

ARKANSAS

Mississippi R.

Red R.

Brazos R.

EXAS

San
Antonio

Rio Grande

GULF OF MEXICO

Chapter One

Francis Alphonse Tucket sat the small mare easily, relaxed in the saddle, his legs loose, the short Lancaster rifle lying casually across his lap, and looked out at the edge of the world.

The prairie stretched away to the horizon. He felt strangely settled, quiet, in a way he had not felt in many months. It had all begun with this very rifle, the beautiful little Lancaster Pa had given Francis on his fourteenth birthday. June 13, 1847. Somehow Pa had managed to hide the rifle with another family in the wagon train that was taking

Francis's family—Ma, Pa, Francis, and Rebecca, who was nine—from Missouri to Oregon. Francis had dropped behind the train to practice with the rifle and he'd been captured. Taken prisoner by Pawnees. It was Jason Grimes the mountain man who had shown up in the Pawnee camp and rescued Francis, taught him to survive as they traveled together. But they had parted ways just the day before, after Grimes's brutal fight with Braid, the Pawnee brave.

Now Francis was on his own. At that moment he felt a kind of peacefulness he had not felt since he'd first taken up with Jason Grimes.

Or boredom, he thought, sitting in the late-afternoon sun. He felt not peacefulness so much as boredom. When he had left the mountain man he had ridden back to meet up with a wagon train waiting at the burned-out hulk of Spot Johnnie's trading post.

They had welcomed him with open arms and had themselves left early the next morning. The wagon master approached him as they were lining out the wagons in the predawn gray light.

"Do you wish to be assigned to a wagon?"

Francis had been looking at the wreckage of Spot Johnnie's post, burned by the Pawnees, in the same direction as the place where he had left Jason Grimes. "What?"

The wagon master smiled and put his hand on Francis's shoulder. "He seemed like a good man . . ."

"Who?"

"The mountain man. He seemed good, a man you would miss being around . . ."

"Well, he wasn't," Francis said curtly. "He wasn't worth spit." He turned to look at the wagon master. "And I don't want to talk about him anymore. What was that about a wagon?"

The wagon master sighed. "Do you wish to be assigned to one?"

Francis looked at them, lumbering along, kids and loose stock running alongside. They were already raising clouds of dust, and there were masses of flies around the horses and oxen—hungry, biting flies. "No, thank you. I'll just free range, if that's all right."

"Maybe you could ride wide and hunt for us as well."

Francis nodded. "I figured on it." He suddenly realized he was talking a lot like Jason Grimes—short, almost cutoff sentences—and he smiled and shrugged. "I mean it seemed the best way for me to help as we go along. Just until we get out farther west and I can get some word about my folks. I'll have to be leaving you then . . ."

"Of course."

The wagon master had ridden off then, riding a Morgan horse that could either pull or ride—a lummox kind of horse, Francis thought—and Francis checked his rifle, made sure the percussion cap was on the nipple tightly, and wheeled the mare toward a ridge off to the north.

If the truth were known, he was glad to be away from the train. He had often been alone in the last months—even when he was with Grimes. Sometimes when they were trapping he was alone for a full day, now and then longer. He had in some ways come to enjoy it. He didn't have to talk to people and it gave him time for thinking.

And he needed to think now. He let the mare pick up the pace to a trot—she wanted to run but he held her back in case he needed speed later—and guided her with his knees until they were on the ridge. Then he eased her over and down the side a bit so he wouldn't be outlined against the sky. It was something Grimes had taught him. Against the sky it was too easy to be seen—either by game or by enemy—and when he was well down from the edge, he swung the mare left and headed west.

He worked his eyes and ears automatically and let his mind start going over the problem.

He felt as if his life had a hole torn in the middle of it—almost the same feeling he'd had when he was taken from the wagon train—and he realized with some surprise that it came from leaving Mr. Grimes.

Francis had not thought they were that close and in some measure hated the man and now this, to feel this . . . this missing the one-armed mountain man.

It made no sense.

The mare slowed and Francis saw her ears perk forward, and she looked suddenly to the right front as a covey of quail jumped from some brush.

Francis was sliding off the side of the horse and halfway to the ground, the rifle cocked and swinging up under the mare's neck when he saw a coyote come out of the brush with a quail in his mouth.

"Could have been anything . . ." He smiled, eased the hammer down to the safety click and remounted. "Anything . . ."

His feet found the stirrups and he kneed the mare into motion once again. The ridge he was riding alongside started to rise and in front ended where it hit a shallow bluff. He could not see over the bluff and moved back up the ridge to the left and made sure there was a place where the wagon train—now moving slowly about two miles to his left and rear—would have room to get through the bluffs.

He still did not ride the mare to the top of the

ridge, but moved up just until his head was high enough to see and then back down.

The bluff ahead beckoned him more. Grimes was, for the moment, out of his thinking—there was something about seeing over the next hill, some need—and he heeled the mare to pick up the pace.

She stepped into an easy canter and climbed the shallow back of the bluff and stopped just as she came on top, and it was here that Francis saw the edge of the world.

Spread out below, reaching away to the horizon and beyond, reaching away west forever, the land, flat and impossibly large, lay before him.

"It . . ." Francis did not finish.

Even the mare had stopped, seemed to be staring at the view, her ears twitching to knock off flies.

"It's too big," he said finally, and realized he meant it. The land was just too big, too big to see, to own—too big to cross. Too big for anything.

It's bad enough on a horse, he thought, how could the wagons, the mile-an-hour wagons, ever hope to cross it? It would take them years . . .

The prairie he had already crossed was enormous—newspapers in the East called it a sea of grass—but Francis had never seen more than a hill or two at a time. This way, from the bluff edge, he could see it all, or a large part of it, and for a moment the bigness kept him from seeing details.

Then the mare stumbled as a gopher hole caved in under her foot, and it snapped Francis back to reality.

In detail the plain before him proved to be not just empty grass, which he'd first thought. Three or four miles to the west, there was a large, dark smudge that seemed to be surrounded by dust clouds. He thought it was trees or low brush, but as he watched, it seemed to move, crawling slowly across the prairie, and he knew it then.

Buffalo. A herd five or six miles across, grazing and kicking up dust.

Or, Francis thought, food for the wagon train. He had never shot a buffalo—with Grimes he had taken deer and antelope, and they'd eaten a lot of beaver meat when they were trapping, but never a buffalo, and he wasn't sure just how to hunt them.

"Do I just ride out there and shoot one?" The mare twitched her ears, listening to his voice. "Is that the way?"

In truth one would not be enough. There were ten wagons—some thirty people—and they would probably want to store meat for the future.

Two, at least, maybe three or four buffalo.

He looked back and to the left and saw the

thread of dust rising from the wagon train. He could go back for them, bring some men from the train with rifles to help. But few of them had horses, were stuck with oxen, and besides he didn't much want to be with the men from the wagons somehow. And it would take two hours to go back and get them.

So his first thought came back. "We'll just have to ride down there and shoot a couple of them."

It proved to be the second biggest mistake of his life.

Chapter Two

The mare took over.

Francis checked the cap on his rifle to insure that it would fire and started the little mare down the front of the bluff to the plain below.

It wasn't quite vertical, but very near it, and the little pony squatted back on her haunches to keep from falling forward.

She was nearly running when she hit the bottom. Francis started to hold her back, but she picked up the pace to a canter, then a full lope, and aimed right at the center of the massive herd.

Things started to happen very fast, and almost none of them were under Francis's control.

The mare flattened her ears and lined out at a dead run. The distance to the herd was diminishing rapidly, almost instantly. One second they were stumbling down the face of the bluff and Francis was checking his rifle and the next they were at the side of the buffalo herd.

The mare stumbled, caught her footing and dived into the herd. Francis had one fleeting image of a bull that seemed to blot out the world and then was immersed in a sea of buffalo, so close they were pressing on the mare's side, rubbing against his leg, bellowing and snorting, raising clouds of dust.

The mare, an Indian pony, had hunted buffalo before. The method used by Indians was to get in close so an arrow or lance could be used, and she remembered her training well.

She took Francis in so close she nearly knocked a large cow over, slamming Francis against her side.

Francis reacted without thinking. He was too close to aim, so he just pressed the muzzle against the shoulder of the cow where he guessed her heart would be, eared the hammer back with his thumb, and fired.

The effect was immediate and startling. The cow went down, caving in and cartwheeling, dead almost before she hit the ground, and the rest of the world blew up.

The herd had been made nervous, at least those near Francis, by the horse running into their midst. But there were wild horses everywhere. The buffalo were used to seeing them all the time, and while the mare running into the herd startled them, they did not really see Francis, only the horse, and would quickly have settled down.

The gunshot ended any chance of peace. They had never heard gunfire before, but they had heard thunder, which meant lightning, and thunder and lightning terrified them.

They panicked, instantly, and within a moment of the panic the entire herd—forty to fifty thousand buffalo, had Francis been able to count them—broke into a thundering stampede.

By this time, Francis and the mare were near the middle of the herd. Francis had half a second to grab the mare's mane, wrap his fingers in the hair and hang on before the herd took her.

It was like being caught in a living river. The buffalo had been aimed south while they grazed and that was the direction they ran. It was impossible to see. Dust rose in an almost solid mass, so thick at times Francis couldn't see the mare's ears, and within moments even the sky was gone.

Without seeing the sun, Francis couldn't tell direction, but it didn't matter. They were caught in the herd, and he let the mare run. She stumbled several times at first, until she caught the stride, but the close press of the buffalo seemed to almost hold her up.

They ran forever.

Or so it seemed. In the thick muck of dirty air, the deafening bellowing of the stampeding buffalo, and the constant push of the animals, Francis forgot time, place, anything and everything, trying to stay on the mare and stay alive.

An hour passed, he was sure of it, and the buffalo kept running. They slowed, or started to, then something would restart them and they'd be off again. The mare settled into the run, covered with sweat, her shoulders pounding. Once the herd seemed to turn, seemed to be wheeling in a huge circle, but he still couldn't see the sun, still couldn't tell what direction they were moving. When they finally stopped, blowing snot and wheezing, the mare staggering with fatigue, Francis didn't have the slightest idea where they were, how far they had come, or in which direction.

They had turned once. He had felt the herd move, swinging around to the left. Or was it right? He sat on the mare, catching his breath while she *whooshed* beneath him, blowing to recover from the run.

Except for the dust, which was rapidly settling, it might not have happened. Buffalo grazed peacefully around him while he looked this way and that, trying to locate himself. His left hand was still clutched in the mare's mane, and he released it, the knuckles aching. He had carried the rifle in his right hand, and he remembered now that it was empty from when he had shot the cow.

He blew dust from the nipple and action and reloaded, sitting on the horse. Powder, patch, and ball, then the ramrod, all done carefully, slowly so as not to bother the buffalo close around him, though they seemed to have forgotten he was there.

With the ball seated firmly on the powder, he took a cap from his possibles sack, pinched it to make it fit tight, and put it on the nipple, eased the hammer slowly to the safety notch.

"There," he said aloud, then winced when a cow standing nearby started at the sudden sound and turned her massive head toward the mare. He had to remember to keep quiet while he worked his way out of the herd.

The problem was which way to go. He guessed they had been running at a good fifteen miles an hour for over an hour.

He thought they had come south. But the dust had covered the sun and now there were low, thick clouds over it, and Francis had no way of knowing direction.

The dust settled as he thought on what to do and with that he saw that he was near the edge of the herd. Scattered groups of buffalo stood between him and clear prairie. He silently nudged the mare into movement—she staggered a bit but kept walking—and moved through the buffalo to the clear area.

The mare was still breathing heavily, and he knew whatever he wanted to do, he would have to give her a rest first—at least four or five hours, better to let her rest all night.

He pulled her up when he was thirty yards past the edge of the herd and dismounted.

He was almost viciously hungry—had not eaten since the previous evening and then had only a tin cup of thin soup and some pan bread the women with the train had made up. There were buffalo nearby and he hadn't had red meat in over a week, so he picked a young bull forty yards off and dropped him with a shot through the neck.

The herd immediately stampeded again as Francis had figured—but he was well clear of them and they ran in a direction away from him. The mare jumped with the shot, but he held tight to her catch rein and there was no problem.

This time he reloaded at once, recapping the nipple before approaching the downed bull, carefully ready to give it another shot if it came at him.

Francis poked the bull with the muzzle of the rifle, but it had been a clean shot, breaking the bull's neck, and it was dead.

Still, some instinct, some wariness made him stand back from the bull, sweep his eyes around, noting every small bush or depression, anywhere anybody could hide. He smelled the air, listened, but there were no strange odors—just the smell of the buffalo—and no sounds but the horn rattle and coughing bellow of the herd, now half a mile away where they had stopped from the run after his shot to kill the bull.

He used the catch rope to make a twist hobble for the mare, took the saddle off, and let her go to graze. She had been hobbled before and moved her front feet in small steps while she fed. Francis would have liked to let her roll, but the hobbles prevented that and he didn't dare let her go loose. She'd take off and he would be afoot.

With the mare settled in for rest and grass, he turned to the dead buffalo. It had fallen straight down, on its chest, its chin furrowed into the dirt.

He had never skinned a buffalo, and when he tried to turn it over to get to the underside, he found it was impossible to move it. The bull was too heavy to even roll over.

For a full minute, he studied the carcass and finally decided he wouldn't be able to skin and clean it as he had done with deer and antelope when he was with Jason Grimes.

As much as it bothered him to waste any part of the animal, he would just have to take meat from the dead bull the best he could. He had sharpened his knife the day before on the small stone he carried in his possibles bag, and he leaned the rifle carefully against the front shoulder of the bull—where he could reach it fast if he needed to—and pulled the knife from the leather scabbard he had on a strap over his shoulder.

He cut down the center of the back, surprised at how easily the skin opened to reveal the yellow-white back-fat and rich meat. The meat was still warm and the thick smell of blood came up into his nose and caught. It made his hunger worse, and he cut a chunk of meat from the back and ate it raw, chewing it only a few bites before swallowing it.

"Good," he mumbled to himself. "So good . . ."

It took him less than half an hour to peel the

hide down both sides and cut a large portion of meat from the hump and tenderloin and set it aside.

Clouds of flies surrounded him. They were part of the buffalo herd anyway, laying eggs in the fresh manure that covered the prairie wherever the herd moved. They were drawn by death and the fresh smell of blood, and within a few moments Francis couldn't see anything through them. They carpeted the meat he set aside, covered his hands, face, were in his eyes.

"Fire . . ." He knew that smoke would drive them away, and he found some dry grass and twigs, poured a tiny amount of powder from his horn in the middle of the pile—noted that the horn was less than half full—and struck a spark with his flint. The spark hit the powder, flashed it, and the heat started the grass and kindling. He quickly added more sticks, dry grass, and some larger pieces he found nearby.

When the fire was high—uncomfortable in the heat of the evening—he propped a six- or seven-pound slab of meat up on sticks close to the flame to cook and went to gather more wood.

He had decided to spend the night and he wanted enough wood to last until morning. The dead wood was sparse, however, and by the time he had made a pile large enough to last it was nearly dark and the smell of the cooked meat was driving him crazy.

He had never been hungrier and he sat by the fire on his rolled-out bedroll, leaning against the saddle and ate the entire piece of meat, taking small sips from his canteen between chunks.

As soon as it was hard dark, coyotes came in to the dead bull—not thirty yards away—and ate. He could see their eyes shining in the light from the fire as they tore at the buffalo but he knew they would not bother him and he paid them no mind.

With his stomach bulging and the warm fire on his face sleep hit him like a wall. Something bothered him and he couldn't quite pin it down— something that he was doing wrong—but the feeling wasn't strong enough to keep him awake.

He pulled his rifle in closer, added wood to the fire, rolled his blanket over to make a cocoon and within minutes was fast asleep.

Chapter Three

"Ahh, see here, Dubs, what fate has provided for us . . . ," a deep, professorial-sounding voice boomed.

It was a dream, Francis was sure of it. It simply wasn't possible that a human voice could be speaking and for a full five seconds he refused to open his eyes and lose the relaxing comfort of sleep.

"Come now, lad. Don't be lazy. We have business afoot. Wake up."

Francis opened his eyes.

At first it didn't matter. The sun was full up and when his lids opened the brightness blinded him.

He blinked, let his eyes adjust, turned away from the sun and opened them again.

He was staring at the dead fire, or more accurately across the fire. There was a man sitting, squatting back on his haunches. He looked old to Francis, over forty, and was so heavily bearded Francis could not see his face for the hair.

But the clothing was more startling. The man was short, almost fat, and dressed in a black suit including a black vest, black boots, black trousers and black frock coat, and a full top hat on his head.

"See, Dubs, the lad awakens." The man smiled—his teeth broken and jagged; a bit of tobacco juice oozed out the side of the lip into the beard and the lines around his black eyes did not match the smile.

Francis slid his hand toward the rifle. Or where the rifle had been. He could not find it.

"See, Dubs, even now he reaches for his weapon. A true child of the frontier." The man spoke to somebody else—Francis couldn't see anybody at first—but kept looking at Francis. The smile widened. Like a snake getting ready to hiss. A hair snake. "I have your rifle—and a nice piece it is, too."

"What . . . who are you?" Francis at last found words. "What are you doing here?"

"Exactly!" The man nodded, waved a filthy finger. "That's exactly what *I* said, wasn't it, Dubs—when we came upon the lad, didn't I say just that? We came over the hill at dawn and I saw you sleeping there and saw your horse and I turned to Dubs and whispered—so as not to disturb your slumbers—and I said: Who is this, and what is he doing here?"

Francis sat up, or tried to. Something heavy, like warm iron, descended on his head and shoulders and pressed him back down. He swiveled his head back and saw that he was looking at a giant—a true giant. It was a man in crude buckskins, so large he seemed to blot out the sun, and Francis saw that the giant had put a hand down to keep him on the blanket.

"Dubs," the man across the fire said by way of introduction. "Isn't he something? There are some who have questioned his humanity, thinking he was of another species—men, I should hasten to add, who are not with us any longer, Dubs having sent them to the nether regions—but I do not question him. I am grateful that he is my partner, my right hand. He is Dubs. I am Courtweiler, although most call me simply Court. And you?"

Francis stared at him. Part of his mind was still trying to awaken and part of him was trying to accept that apparently these men meant to harm him. If they had been friendly they would not have taken his rifle. He realized that what had bothered him last night was his acting like an amateur, a greenhorn. He should have placed his bedroll well away from the fire, hidden so he would have time to react if enemies came. Stupid. Well, nothing for it now. He had to buy time, time to think, time to come up with a plan. "Francis," he said. "My name is Francis."

"Ahh—a proper name, that. Francis. I would have liked to have been named Francis but my ancestors came into it and I had to take the family name. Courtweiler isn't bad, but Francis—now that's a name, isn't it, Dubs?"

Francis looked up again and if the giant was listening at all he gave no indication. He held Francis down with one hand while staring out across the prairie.

"It was a stroke of good fortune coming upon you this way," Courtweiler added. "For us, that is. Not so good for you."

"What do you mean?" Francis looked at his rifle, which was across the fire on the ground leaning against Courtweiler's leg while he squatted. He couldn't reach it. And his possibles bag and knife were somewhere in back of him—he'd never get to them before Dubs landed on him.

"I mean, Francis, that we have a specific need for just about everything you have. Our equipment has run into the ground and we aren't halfway to that golden coast we aspire to. I'm afraid we're going to have to relieve you of your belongings."

"My belongings?"

Courtweiler nodded. "Exactly. Gun, horse, saddle—essentially everything. I think I could even fit into that buckskin shirt."

"My clothes, too?"

"Except your pants. I think we'll leave those in the interests of propriety. But everything else. And I don't want you to think I'm ungrateful. Indeed, if you will turn and look," he made a sign to Dubs, who stepped back and let Francis rise, "you will see that I am in desperate straits indeed. Even my mule suffers."

Francis rose to his knees and looked to the rear where an old mule, so skinny its ribs stuck out inches, stood with its head hanging nearly to the ground. On its back was a blanket worn until there were holes through it, no saddle, and instead of a bridle a loop went around the lower jaw. The miracle, Francis thought, was that the mule had gotten this far.

"You see what I mean." Courtweiler pointed to

the mule. "Dubs prefers to go afoot, and by the third day will outrun a horse. But given as I am to more intellectual pursuits and less of the physical I need to ride. And so we must have your horse."

"I have kin," Francis said. "Just over that rise. They'll be looking for me . . ."

Courtweiler shook his head. "Dissembling won't help, my boy. We came from there. There are no people there, no tracks, nothing. I do not know how you arrived here but let me assure you, there is nobody close to help you."

"I'll die if you leave me here with nothing."

Courtweiler sighed. "Indeed. There is that possibility. Still, life on the frontier is very hard and we must expect these little setbacks and somehow muddle on, don't you agree? Now, please take off that shirt before I have to ask Dubs to assist you . . ."

Francis hesitated, saw Dubs move and decided not to anger the huge man. He shrugged out of his shirt, felt the morning coolness on his skin.

"Off the blanket, please."

Francis moved from the blanket and Dubs snaked it off the ground and rolled it up in one fluid motion and stood again, still, waiting.

"And now, Francis, as fruitful as it has been to meet you, I'm afraid we must be off . . ."

Dubs had already caught the mare—Francis

could not believe they had done all this without awakening him—and they saddled her, left the mule standing and rode off, Courtweiler holding Francis's rifle across his lap as they rode away, headed west while Francis sat next to a dead buffalo, a nearly dead mule, and watched them go.

──Chapter Four──

For a time Francis stood in a kind of shock. He could still see them when they were a mile away, heading toward the tail end of the buffalo herd, and then two miles, small dots on the prairie.

My life, he thought. I'm watching my life leave. For that time he couldn't, or wouldn't, think. He knew there were bad men in some of the wagon trains, had heard that some of them were kicked out of the trains and he thought Courtweiler and Dubs might be two of those men. Perhaps they had stolen, or worse, and been forced to leave.

It didn't matter. Francis shook his head to clear his thinking. What mattered was that he was in the middle of God knew where, did not have any sure idea of which way to go to find the wagon train he had left the day before, was nearly naked with no weapons and no tools, and his life, his horse and rifle and all that he needed to live, was riding over a rise two miles away. That was what mattered.

As he thought, Dubs and Courtweiler vanished, hidden by the land, and Francis looked around, half expecting somebody to step forward and say it was a joke, or to help him.

There was nobody and he frowned, thinking. There was an answer here somewhere, something they had said, or Courtweiler had said. What was it?

Was it about Dubs? Dubs didn't use a horse. He just trotted alongside, moving forward in a step shuffle—he looked almost exactly like a bear moving—and he easily kept up with the mare.

Something about the horse, some comment. What was it? Oh yes, by the third day he could outrun a horse. Wasn't that it? Francis looked north again. He guessed that north was the direction he'd have to walk—twenty miles or more—to find the wagon train. But it was only a guess. If the buffalo herd had turned in the dust while they ran—and he had no idea if they had or not—he would be wrong and miss the train. If he missed the train he would almost certainly die—unless he ran into Indians who would help him. The problem was that some of the Indians might *not* help him.

Three days, he thought again. And there it was—the answer. If that big ox could outrun a horse in three days Francis should be able to do it in two. Wearing nothing but moccasins and leather leggings he should be able to do it in one.

He should be able to keep up with them. That was the answer. He would follow them and wait, hang back where they couldn't see him and watch and wait and maybe, when they slept, he could turn it around—do what they had done to him.

He shrugged, loosened his legs from days of riding and when he turned he saw the mule. For half a second he thought of trying it, riding the mule bareback until he played out and went down. But the animal was too far gone—looked out on his feet—and Francis shook his head.

"Sorry, mule—you'll have to stay alone." The wolves would come for him, Francis knew. It was pure luck they hadn't found the dead buffalo yet. Coyotes had come during the night but not the wolves—huge, gray, slab-sided beasts that followed the herds of buffalo to get the old and sick and young. They would make short work of the mule and Francis felt sorry for it; to have come this far just to get torn apart by wolves seemed a cruel fate.

But again he shook his head. His own situation wasn't much better. He'd never heard of wolves attacking men but he would have felt much more comfortable about it if he'd had a rifle or even a knife.

"Enough . . ."

He started off, following the mare's tracks in a shuffle that approximated Dubs's—his toes in, feet almost not leaving the ground.

There was still morning coolness, but the sun was well up and felt warm on his back, and inside of fifteen minutes he was covered with sweat. He watched the tracks moving through the torn ground where the buffalo had gone, fixed on them and kept up the pace for an hour—he figured maybe five miles—when he breasted a rounded rise and could see out ahead again for several miles.

He stopped, catching his breath, and squinted, trying to see ahead as far as possible. For a full minute he stood, could see nothing except small stands of buffalo—two here, three there—and then way off, so small it seemed like bits of dust on his eyes, he saw them. He thought he might have gained—he guessed them to be three miles away— and it was unmistakably the mare with Courtweiler on top and Dubs trotting alongside.

"Good . . ." He took another deep breath and was just ready to step off into the shuffle again when he heard a sound to his rear and turned to see the mule standing there, its head down, eating grass.

"You followed me?"

The mule twitched one ear but kept eating and Francis shook his head. He'd heard that mules were tougher than horses, but this was an old mule and it didn't seem possible that it could have stayed with him, or that it would want to.

"Well, it's good to have company . . ."

He set off again in the easy trot and when he looked over his shoulder he saw the mule take one last bite, raise its head and start off, moving in a shambling, fast walk-trot that easily kept up with Francis.

He must be made of iron, Francis thought. Iron and leather.

He thought of slowing some—he didn't want to catch up to them enough for them to know he was following and the mule, which stood taller than Francis, would show from a long way. But he figured he would slow naturally as the day went on and he didn't want to fall far enough back to lose them.

So he kept the same pace, trotting along. Another hour passed and he saw them again, estimated that he hadn't gained and from then on there was nothing but running.

At first he grew tired. At midday when the sun was overhead, it seemed that he would drop. He was viciously thirsty and it would have stopped him —sweating without water—but he found a small spring on the side of a mud buffalo wallow and he drank enough to slake his thirst. It restored his energy and picked him up enough that the ache in his legs and thighs turned to a dull burn and then, finally, disappeared entirely.

By midafternoon he felt as if he could run forever. The exhaustion had gone, was replaced by a lifting of spirits that almost made him happy—or as happy as a half-naked, unarmed man in the middle of the wilderness can be.

The mule was still with him, shambling along, and as evening approached he found another spring and drank and the mule drank with him, next to him, and Francis realized that he'd told the truth earlier; it *was* nice to have company, even if it was just a mule.

A very old, very tough mule. And as it turned out, a very dangerous mule. Just before dark Francis stopped. He felt sure Courtweiler and Dubs would camp for the night and he didn't want to run up to them.

As soon as he stopped the wolves found them. It

was not a full pack, just three young ones. But they were still dangerous, at least to the mule, and there was little Francis could do. They came in on the mule, who stood, his ears laid back and his head down. Francis threw rocks at them but they merely growled and didn't run and grew bolder with each moment and one of them, the largest, finally had enough of waiting and went for the mule's rear end.

It was his last act on earth.

Francis had never seen anything like it. The mule raised one back hoof when the wolf made his move—Francis thought later it was like cocking a rifle—and kicked so hard and fast Francis couldn't see it move. One instant the wolf was making an attack and the next the whole front of his head was caved in and he hit the ground a full ten feet back, absolutely stone dead. He didn't even twitch.

The other wolves saw it happen; one of them went over to the dead wolf and smelled the body, then looked at the mule, shook himself, and the two trotted off into the evening.

Francis watched them go and smiled at the mule. "Well, if I can't have a rifle or knife you're the next best thing—like a cannon."

He stood close to the mule. In the evening the heat of the day was going fast and he had perspired all day. A chill came into him and he found that by standing against the mule while it ate he felt warmer, and listening to the mule pull grass and chew somehow made it more peaceful, protected, and let him think on his next move.

It would be dark soon. He didn't know how close he might be to them, or even if they were going to stop for the night—although he somehow couldn't see them traveling hard—but he thought they might be fairly close. A mile or less.

Just before the wolves had come he had moved to the top of a low knoll and scanned ahead. A mile to the west there was a streambed thick with low trees running along its side, and if it were his choice he would camp there where there was wood for fire and water for the horse.

He leaned against the mule—which was still, and Francis guessed would forever be eating—and absorbed the warmth from the bony shoulder and waited.

Finally, when it was pitch-dark he left the mule and climbed the knoll again, looked in the direction of the streambed. For a second there was nothing. Then he saw it.

A flicker, then, when his eyes locked on it he could see the full glow of a campfire.

He had found them.

Now all he had to do was wait.

Chapter Five

It was a wonderful dream. He had dreamt many times since Braid had taken him from the wagon train and he had trapped with Jason Grimes, most often of his parents. Some of them were night-mares, some were happy. But this one was best of all.

He dreamt about beans. His mother had a large pot of beans on the stove and she had put a ham hock in them so the fat and taste went into the beans and it had cooked to perfection, and his mother had ladled some into a bowl and put a chunk of butter on top and was handing it to him, just handing it to him . . .

His eyes opened.

He had no real way to tell time but there was a sliver of a moon and it had risen to halfway across the sky. He guessed that half the night was gone and if they were ever going to sleep they would be by now.

Francis had been sitting on a rock dozing and he rose, stretched, rubbed his arms and set off in the dark. The day's run had worn a hole in his right moccasin and it kept scooping dirt which he shook out periodically. When he stopped to shake his moccasin the third time he turned and saw that the mule was with him.

It is one thing to sneak into camp and try to steal my stuff back alone, he thought, looking at the mule. It is something else again to do it with a whole mule walking in back of me.

There was a very real danger. If the mare smelled the mule she might whicker or whinny and the sound would awaken the two men. If they were asleep. If he could get close enough. If. If.

He couldn't stop the mule if it wanted to follow him and he finally decided to chance it. He would need luck but the way it was going he would need all the luck in the world anyway. He might as well push it.

He turned and trotted off again, sensed rather than heard the mule following him, clumping along.

Things looked dramatically different in the dark. Twice he saw coyotes, once a single wolf that moved off into the darkness, and several times he passed buffalo. A rattlesnake buzzed as he passed, but it was well away from his path and stopped as soon as he was by. The streambed didn't show at all at first, and then when he thought he would never get to it he was suddenly in the trees and low brush that grew along the watercourse.

He stopped, listening, but could hear only the sound of the mule eating in back of him. The mule ate every time he stopped, had been eating all day every chance it got, but the sound wasn't loud and after a moment he moved on.

There was no fire to see now—which was a good sign and he hoped meant both men were asleep. But it made things difficult as far as finding the camp. He didn't want to blunder into them but he was running out of time. It would begin to get light soon—within the hour—and they would awaken.

His nose finally did the trick. As he turned, looking for some glow of embers and trying to see the mare in the dark, he smelled the smoke from the nearly dead fire.

Left, to the left it was stronger and he moved that way and hadn't gone twenty yards when he found them.

It was hard to see in the darkness but he made out the shape of the mare off across the fire. She either did not see the mule or didn't care and was silent.

The men were harder to locate. He stood for a full three minutes studying the campsite and finally saw them against the dark brush around the fire clearing.

Dubs was to his left, lying on his side with no blanket over him, sleeping like a great bear, and Courtweiler was across the fire pit, on his back with Francis's saddle for a pillow and Francis's blanket and bedroll for covers.

They were both snoring, but so lowly that Francis had to concentrate to hear it and he smiled. Good. They were asleep. Now if he could locate his rifle. None of this would work without the rifle —actually both rifles. He needed his and Dubs's. Two men, two shots.

He had no real plan except to get his rifle and force them to give his equipment back.

There. His Lancaster rifle was next to Courtweiler, the muzzle across the saddle by his head. Close. Maybe too close.

How would it go? He tried to imagine it, plan it.

He would get his rifle, then cover them and somehow get Dubs's rifle.

And what, shoot them if they made a try for him? Shoot them? He hesitated. He'd never shot a person, or at least didn't think he had. He had aimed at an Indian who was attacking him, but he thought Jason Grimes had done the shooting and he'd missed, or maybe wounded him.

On the other hand they had left him for dead, these two men. They could easily kill him, and would if they got a chance.

That's how it might play. He'd get his rifle, try to get Dubs's weapon, and shoot the big man if he had to. He took a breath, held it, worked his way softly and quietly around the side of the fire until he was standing over Courtweiler.

He squatted, reached forward, and gently, so gently wrapped his fingers around the stock of the rifle just ahead of the hammer and lifted it away from the saddle, stood back with it.

I missed you, he thought, holding the little Lancaster. He felt to make sure there was a cap on the nipple, then eared the hammer back slowly, holding the trigger so it wouldn't make a clicking sound when it cocked.

So far so good. He stood back and away and moved around to Dubs. The giant's rifle was next to him on the ground and Francis leaned down carefully and reached for it and happened to look at Dubs's face and nearly screamed out loud.

Dubs's eyes were wide open staring at him. Even in the pale light from the partial moon Francis could see the whites, the glare from them, and he thought, I am dead, this instant I am dead.

But Dubs didn't move and when he peered closer—something it took his whole heart to do— he saw that the eyes weren't truly on him, were just open.

Dubs slept with his eyes open.

It was enough to stop Francis. He stared at the man, moved his hands back and forth in front of his eyes, and there was no reaction. Nothing.

But the delay was nearly fatal. He had a firm grip on Dubs's rifle, was lifting it away when he heard a small sound in back of him, a rustling, and something grabbed his hair.

"Ahh, it's you, Francis. How good of you to call . . ."

Francis tore free but the sound had awakened Dubs and both men came at him. He somehow didn't remember that he was holding two rifles and could shoot them. And in any event it was all happening too fast.

Dubs came out of sleep instantly, animalistically,

ready for battle. He rolled to his feet, towered over Francis, reached for him from the left while Court-weiler reached from the right.

They would have him. In a second or less they would have him. He fell backward over the dead fire and his fall saved him.

Dubs was nearly on top of him but overshot when he reached for Francis. The hulk went over Francis, a good two feet beyond, and ran squarely into the mule, who had been following Francis as before.

There was a sound like someone splitting a wa-termelon with an ax and Dubs dropped as if he'd been shot with a howitzer. The mule swung a bit to the side, aimed quickly and caught Courtweiler dead in the middle of the stomach with another well-aimed kick and Courtweiler went down wheezing for breath. Suddenly Francis was the only human able to function.

He stood quickly, aimed the rifle at the two men, but it wasn't necessary. Dubs had taken it directly in the head, and while he was still breath-ing it would clearly be some time before he regained consciousness. Courtweiler still couldn't breathe and was only half conscious himself.

"I guess you must have been hard on the mule," Francis said aloud as he gathered his gear. "I hear they've got good memories . . ."

He moved from the fire pit to the mare, caught her and led her back by the camp to saddle, watching the two men all the while, the Lancaster still cocked and ready to fire. In the east there was a gray softness to the dark and he worked quickly. He wanted to be well away from these two before they could react, and he tied his bedroll in place in back of the saddle and laid his shirt across his lap as he mounted—he didn't want to lower his guard long enough to pull the shirt on over his head. He had taken what equipment there was that belonged to the two men as well and he draped it across the mare's neck.

"You're . . . leaving . . . us . . . like . . . this?" Courtweiler gasped while he spoke, still fighting for breath.

Francis nodded. "You're lucky I don't put a ball in you." He used his legs to back the mare away from the camp. Before turning her he said softly: "Don't come at me again. I won't be so easy to catch off guard and I *will* shoot you."

Courtweiler said nothing and Francis turned and rode away, smiling to himself when he saw the mule take one last bite of bunch grass and rush to follow him.

When he was half a mile from the men he stopped and pulled his shirt on, lashed the extra rifle—which turned out to be a crude version of a

Hawkens, with what appeared to be a half-inch bore—to the saddle horn so it hung down the mare's side and tied his canteen and the one he'd taken from Courtweiler so they balanced one on either side.

Then he set off again, the sun coming over his back. He needed miles in case they decided to follow him as he had done with them so he heeled the mare and picked up the speed, the mule shambling along in back.

He caught himself humming in time to the mare's movement and smiled openly. Where he'd been alone he now had two friends—one of them, the mule, a definitely powerful friend. Where he'd been without anything he now had two canteens, two rifles, two possibles bags, and an extra horn almost full of powder.

He was rich.

Now all he had to do was find the wagon train and get out to Oregon.

Chapter Six

In one sense his situation hadn't improved. He really didn't know where he was, or which direction to take to find the train.

He decided to head west and cut north when the country to the north looked like easier going. Now it seemed to be made up of bluffs, some fifteen miles distant, and he didn't want to try work the mare and mule over them.

He rode west and angled north slightly, figuring if he missed the train at least he might hit the tracks they left going by.

The riding was easy, especially after the run the day before. His legs still ached and he kept falling asleep in the saddle, particularly when the afternoon sun began cooking his back.

In midafternoon he ran into a small stream where he watered the mare. The mule drank as well—it was actually looking better all the time—and Francis decided to run in the water for a mile or two to help throw the tracks off.

He set the mare in the middle of the stream and was surprised to see the mule mimic her, stepping into the water and putting his feet nearly exactly where the mare stepped.

He left the stream in half an hour, continuing west and slightly north, and he was just thinking he might catch the train tonight, thinking maybe they would have some fresh bread made, or stew, or maybe coffee with sugar in it . . . just letting himself dream of food when the rain hit.

He hadn't noticed the clouds. They had come up in patches, blown away while he rode-dozed, and somehow they had come together again without his realizing it.

At first it sprinkled and he hunched his shoulders and took it. But in a short time the clouds became more dense and the rain came harder and then it roared.

He would have gotten off the mare but there was

nowhere to go, no shelter. He was soaked instantly, and getting cold and hoping it was a short storm and would stop, but it didn't. It rained in a wide belt of dark storm clouds for close to three hours, poured like somebody was dumping giant buckets.

At one point it came down so hard he could not see the mare's head only three feet away, and he lost sight of the mule for the entire storm. He put both powder horns inside his shirt to keep the powder dry but everything else was soaked.

When it stopped, close to evening again, he dismounted and unsaddled the mare and hobbled her. In the evening light he spread his blanket on some brush to dry and by reaching up under the side of a streambed above the water he found some dry bits of wood protected from the rain.

He used a tiny portion of powder and his striker to make a fire, fed it with more small bits of dry wood until the heat could dry out some larger pieces and settled in for the night. There was no food—not in his own possibles bag and not in the one he'd taken from Courtweiler and Dubs—but there was a small metal pot and he made hot water and sipped it, pretending it was coffee with sugar.

"At least," he said aloud to the mule, which was standing nearby while the mare grazed off a bit on her hobble, "any tracks we've left are wiped out. If they're following us they'll never find us . . ."

He trailed off as what he said sank into his thinking. It was true that any tracks he'd left would be gone and he would be impossible to find.

But that held true for *all* tracks. His tracks would have been wiped out by the storm. But not only his tracks.

The wagon tracks would be gone as well. Even if he hit their trail he wouldn't find their tracks. He wouldn't find the wagons unless he ran into the train itself, and the chances of that happening—hitting them exactly right in the enormous area of the plains—were somewhere on the scale of finding a needle in a haystack.

He prepared for bed, rolled in a damp blanket well away from the fire—he would not make the same mistake twice—with the mule standing near him, and as he felt the exhaustion of the past two days take him, he could not stop thinking the word *lost*.

I am lost.

Chapter Seven

After a time, a day, a month, years—a time he could not really measure—it did not seem as if he were moving but that he was standing in one place and the prairie rolled by beneath the mare.

He arose and left camp without a fire, stretching the stiffness out of his bones while he saddled. He remembered that, getting up. And then mounting in the coolness and being hungry. But after that everything blended into a sameness that defied memory. He kept the rising sun on the back of his right shoulder and rode, and rode, and rode . . .

It was the prairie, the grass sea, and it was endless. He began to look for things to break the monotony. A buffalo here, a jackrabbit there, but he had left the area where the buffalo herd passed and ate the grass down, and the grass here was so high—at times even with his waist sitting up on the mare—he could see nothing smaller than a full-sized bull buffalo.

A day passed. He left in the morning and evening came and it was time to stop and there was no change. He found a spring—there were dozens of them, seeping into wallows—and refilled his canteens and let the mare drink. The mule took a sip and at once began eating, and watching him eat made Francis's hunger worse.

It was going on two days since he'd eaten from the bull, two days and many hard miles and he was so hungry his stomach seemed to be caving in.

He drank large quantities of water to swell his stomach but it didn't help.

He would have to find something, hunt something. The mare was hobbled and the mule seemed to have changed his loyalties and was content to stay with her. Francis eyed the sun. There were probably two or three hours until hard dark, and around the spring there were dozens of fresh deer tracks.

They probably came in for water in the evenings

before heading back into the grass to eat and avoid the wolves.

He checked the cap on his rifle and put his possibles bag over his shoulder and headed into the grass.

It was like stepping into a different world. On the mare he had been above it, but now the grass was as tall as he was and he couldn't see more than a few feet and it was alive with sound.

He moved slowly, listening intently. There was a constant scurrying of mice and rabbits and twice he heard things move, heavy things, and he thought they were probably deer and he had decided to give it up, that it wasn't going to work, when he came upon the trail.

It was made by deer coming in to water and the ground was churned to powder by their sharp hooves. Francis stopped, studied the trail and decided the best way to hunt in the grass was to sit next to it and wait for something to come along. He certainly wouldn't have any luck blundering around the way he had been doing.

He found a small clearing—more a dent back into the grass than a true clearing—and he settled in and down, sitting with his thumb on the hammer of the rifle and his finger on the trigger.

He hadn't been there five minutes when a fawn came past. It was growing out of spots but still small and in back of her came her mother, a young doe, sleek and fat from the grass and leaves.

He could have shot either of them easily but something wouldn't let him fire at the fawn and the thought of killing her mother was just as bad. As it happened his hesitation was rewarded. Within minutes a young buck, three points on each side, stepped cautiously down the trail not five feet from Francis.

Francis waited until his head was past, raised the rifle, cocked it and fired, aiming just in back of the shoulder where he knew the heart lay.

The noise was deafening in the grass, seemed to fill the space around him, and he blinked. When he opened his eyes the buck was gone and he stood slowly, reloaded and listening, trying to locate it by sound, but all he could hear was a ringing in his ears from the crack of the rifle.

The buck hadn't gone far. Francis's shot had been accurate, and it had taken only three steps before settling into the grass with its head laid back on its shoulders.

He poked it with the muzzle of the rifle as he had done the buffalo, but it was gone and he set to work at once, gutting the deer and skinning it. This time he would not be so wasteful.

He took the back meat and tenderloin, then the

meat from the back legs, leaving the bones for the coyotes. It took him only a few minutes to make a fire from some dead brush near the wallow, and he cooked strips of venison hung over green sticks and ate them when they were still nearly raw.

He thought there'd been a lot of meat on the buck, but he ate over fifteen pounds, ate until his stomach hurt with it, ate until he couldn't get another bite in his mouth, and by that time there were only another ten or so pounds of meat.

This he cut into strips—the way he'd seen his Indian "mother" do when he was a captive—and hung them over the fire but away from the flames to dry them out and keep the flies away while the meat hardened into a kind of quick jerky.

He built the fire up some to keep it going for a while and took his bedroll back in the grass a good twenty yards from the fire, carefully closing the grass back in place as he moved. After his bedroll was spread out, he sat quietly for fifteen minutes listening, his mouth open, holding his breath again and again to hear anything that might mean a possible problem. But all he heard were the scurryings of small rodents, two coyotes already working at the deer carcass, and the sounds of the mule and the mare eating nearby.

Finally satisfied he put both rifles by his side,

checked them to be sure they were loaded and capped correctly one more time, pulled the blanket over the top to keep the night chill out, blinked once and was sound asleep.

Chapter Eight

The next morning was different. He started right, ate some meat and drank water, made sure all his gear was finally dry, and was moving well before dawn.

Morning light revealed that the line of bluffs to the north had come to a shallow end and he swung straight north on the off chance that he would run into the wagon train.

It was a beautiful day and the mare was frisky, so he let her run for a mile to burn it out, loping easily, and was amazed to see the mule keep up handily.

"Whoa . . ." He held the mare down and studied the mule. It had filled out beautifully in just two days of constant eating and wasn't breathing hard though it had loped a mile. "You actually look younger," Francis said aloud. "Maybe we can rig a pack saddle up later and use you."

He set off again, holding the mare to a fast walk, his eyes sweeping the grass in front of them, and in two hours he found a track.

Actually, if he'd blinked he would have missed it. It wasn't a track so much as a faint line across the prairie, heading west, a blemish in the grass that could only be seen when the light was exactly right.

It was not left by a train—probably by a single wagon—but it was something, a track, which was better than he'd had before, and he turned to follow it. It must have been made before the rain, and the grass the wagon had run over had been broken enough to stay at least partially down. When Francis dismounted and felt down in the grass he could feel slight indentations in the prairie sod, barely half an inch deep.

He remounted and followed the track, which seemed to go west by slightly south, and tried not to hope.

It was only midday, but by late afternoon the tracks seemed to have faded more and he was having trouble following them. It had struck him as odd that a single wagon would come out here alone, but there was something drawing him on and he decided to give it another hour or two before turning back to the west.

The country was the same. Rolling flat, or what seemed to be flat with shallow dips into more flatness. He thought he could see for miles, and he couldn't see anything like a wagon, and at last he decided to end the run and cut north again.

His turn to the north took him onto a low rise, and at the top of the rise he happened to glance left and something caught his eye.

He stopped and studied it. Way off, over a mile, there was something round sticking up out of the grass. It wasn't white, quite, but a gray color. A gray spot and he realized it was tarp, canvas, and that he was looking at the top of a covered wagon.

The mare turned west again without his meaning to turn her—answering pressure from his knees—and he nudged her into a fast walk.

If it was a wagon it would have people. And if there were people they might know where they were, or where the main wagon train was.

But as he drew closer he felt a strangeness about the wagon. It was stopped dead, as if camped. But he could see no stock, no sign of life, and there wasn't any smoke from a cook fire.

He stopped a hundred yards from the wagon and sat on the mare, his thumb on the hammer of the rifle. "Hello!"

No answer.

"Hello at the wagon—is anybody there?"

Silence. For a second he thought he heard a small sound, almost a whimper, but it could have come from the mare or the mule breathing.

"I'm coming in and I'm friendly!"

Still he sat, tensed, waiting for any sign of movement or threat. Again he thought he heard a small sound, but it was so soft he could not be sure and other than that, nothing.

The mule ended it. He had been standing in back of the mare, but he saw the wagon and decided to investigate and walked past the mare and went up to the wagon.

Nothing happened, and Francis took it as a good sign and thumped his heels against the mare's ribs and moved to the wagon.

"Hello!" he said again, but there was no answer. He could find no sign of life until he came to the rear of the wagon and looked inside.

There were two children sitting on a quilt, a girl and a boy, their eyes wide with fright. The girl was eight or nine, wearing a sunbonnet with most of the stiffener out of the brim so it drooped. The boy was five or six. Both of them were blond and covered with freckles. As Francis stared at them—finding children was the last thing he had expected to do—the girl made a sound, a cry, and Francis recognized it as the sound he had heard.

"Where are your folks?" Francis looked around the wagon and could see nothing. "And how did the wagon get here? Where are your animals?"

The boy jumped at the sound and stuck a thumb in his mouth and started sucking. The girl seemed startled as well but seemed to have more spunk than the boy.

"Are you a savage?" she asked. "Are you one of them savages?"

Francis shook his head. "I don't think so. My name is Francis. What's yours?"

She relaxed. "I'm Charlotte, but folks all called me Lottie. This is Billy. Of course, it's William and not Billy, but Billy is the short way of saying William just like Lottie is short for Charlotte, and ain't that the strangest thing? Who would think Billy would come from William instead of it being Willy or just plain Will . . ."

Francis held up his hand. "Easy, easy."

"I like to talk," she said. "Sometimes it gets away from me a little."

Francis nodded.

"It's like there's a place in me full of words and when I open the door to the place they just start coming and I can't seem to stop . . ."

Again Francis held up his hand. "We have other things to talk about now. Where are your folks?"

"Folk," she said. "It was just Pa. Ma went on must have been two years ago when some croup came and took her. Pa decided to go West, but he got the water sickness and they made us leave the train."

"Water sickness?" Francis stopped her again. "You mean cholera?"

She nodded. "That's the one. He was taken sick, and we came out here so he could get well except that he didn't. Get well I mean. It started to take him down, and he left us with some flour and biscuits that he made and took off walking until he got over it so we wouldn't take the sickness from him."

"How long ago was that?" Cholera, Francis thought. Cholera. They said it came from drinking bad water, but nobody was sure and he wondered if he could catch it just by being close to the children. "When did he go off?"

"It's been two days and a little more now." She hesitated, and Francis saw a tear come down her cheek and saw that Billy was crying as well, and perhaps had been the whole time. "He ain't coming back, is he?"

Some died in a day, Francis had heard. Some had a fever in the morning and were dead by noon. The man had gone off to die alone to protect his children, although leaving them alone in the prairie was close to a death sentence. Pushing the sick ones out was the only protection wagon trains had, getting the sick ones away from the unsick people. But it still seemed a brutal thing to Francis, pushing these children out with their sick father when they obviously weren't sick, making them go it alone.

Except, Francis thought, they weren't alone. Not now. He couldn't leave them. They wouldn't last a week. And they weren't sick, or didn't appear to be.

"Wait here," he said. "I'm going to look around a bit. I'll be back."

He left them in the wagon and started searching out and around the wagon. He was looking for the father on the off chance that he had survived—some had, he knew, although it left them sickly—and he didn't want to leave the man here if he wasn't dead.

He found the father on the fourth circle around the wagon. He had gone a good distance—two hundred yards—before settling into the grass. Francis read the sign. He was flat on his back and very dead, although the coyotes and wolves hadn't been at him yet. His arms were at his sides and he had a peaceful look on his face—if, Francis thought, dead people can have any look—and it looked like he'd been sitting and just laid back when death came.

I should bury him, Francis thought, but he knew he couldn't. He shouldn't even be this close and he backed the mare away shaking his head. He hated to leave but the sickness could still be here, still be around the body, and he didn't want to take any chances. He'd have to leave the body.

He went straight back to the wagon where the children still sat inside on the quilt.

"Did you find Pa?" Lottie asked.

Francis didn't answer the question but instead scanned the prairie around the wagon again. "Didn't you have horses or oxen when you came?"

Lottie nodded. "Two horses. Buck and Booger. But Pa he let them loose just before he got bad sick and something run them off."

Wolves, Francis thought. They're probably dead and if not they're so far away I could never find them.

"What are we going to do?" Lottie asked, and Francis thought, That's it, that's it exactly, as Courtweiler would have said. What could he do?

Suddenly he was not alone. He had two children

to care for and nothing else had changed. He didn't know where he was or where to go, didn't know anything except now there were three of them instead of just one.

He shook his head. It would have to be taken a step at a time and one thing was sure, they couldn't stay here.

"Get your stuff together," he told Lottie. "And Billy's, too. We're going to go."

"Where?" Lottie asked.

Good question, Francis thought—and I don't have the tiniest part of an answer. But he smiled, a smile he didn't really feel, and pointed with his chin.

"West," he said. "We're going to go West . . ."

Chapter Nine

Again the mule saved him.

It was one thing to say they were going to go West, something else again to do it. The children were small, but they could not have all three ridden the mare and they couldn't have walked. Francis could have walked and led them on the mare and was thinking of doing just that when he saw the mule standing by the wagon.

"Could you carry them?" he said aloud and Lottie misunderstood, thought he was talking to her.

"You mean me? Could I carry Billy? Well, for a little ways . . ."

"No, no. I was talking to the mule."

"The mule? You were talking to a mule? Do they know how to talk? They look so dumb the way they just stand all the time except this one seems to eat more than anything I've seen . . ."

"Is there a halter in the wagon?"

"Yeah. Pa he kept extra ones for the horses but I'm not sure he'd want you taking them . . . Oh. I guess it doesn't matter, does it?"

She climbed into the wagon and came out in a moment with a halter. Francis tied the mare to the wagon wheel and dismounted, walked up to the mule with the halter and was surprised when the mule stuck his head through it and let him buckle it in place.

"I thought mules were s'posed to be fractious," Lottie said. "Pa he said mules were all the time being fractious but your mule seems to be a right nice fellow. Time was I saw a mule belonged to our neighbor, her name was Nancy and she had red hair and lived a mile away down a rocky road and worked all the time. Anyway she had a mule name of Plover and he could kick so fast he'd kick a rock if you threw it at his back end . . ."

Francis let her talk and used a rope to tie a folded blanket from the wagon on the mule's back. It was makeshift at best, but it would give them something to sit on.

He had thought fleetingly of trying to harness the mule and the mare to pull the wagon, but it was too heavy and they were much too lightweight to take the load for very long. And besides, he didn't want to be encumbered with a wagon. They might hit rough country where a wagon couldn't go.

There were other things he took from the wagon. Another rifle, and under the seat wrapped in a grease-stained sack of soft leather, he found a .44 Colt's cap and ball revolver. He wasn't much on handguns—they were mostly inaccurate and didn't have any range or punch—but it held six balls and he thought there might come a time when he would need to shoot without reloading so he took it, along with a bullet mold and a box of caps and a full flask of powder. There was some flour—he ate half a handful raw—and some matches and salt and a cast-iron Dutch oven with a lid. All of this he placed in a canvas bag he'd found in the wagon, which he hung on the mule.

He took two more blankets and the quilt to make a bedroll for the children, cut a large piece of canvas from the top of the wagon for a tent or lean-to, rolled them all and tied them across the mule's shoulders and stood back to look at it. It was bulky, but light, and the two children together wouldn't make half a man—they were skinny as well as small—and he thought the mule would not have any trouble carrying them.

He led the mule up to the rear of the wagon and reached in, loaded Billy and Lottie onto the mule's back. The mule took the load easily and didn't flinch or buck, for which Francis was thankful.

Then he mounted the mare, took the mule's lead rope in his hand and left the wagon. He did not look back for some time and when he did the wagon was a spot in the endless grass and Lottie was looking straight at him. But the boy had somehow turned around on the mule and was sitting backward, sucking his thumb, still silent, staring at the wagon.

Chapter Ten

The Indians found them in midafternoon.

Or, in reality, Francis and the Indians found each other.

Francis and the children started from the wagon about noon, working west and slightly north. He could think of no reason for the northerly movement except that it seemed right, a hunch, and he decided to follow it, hoping to cut a wagon train—the one he'd left or the one that had set the children and their father out. But he understood there was little chance.

The boredom set back in. There were long silences while they rode. Francis thought of his family, his mind triggered by the two children with him. Ma. Pa. His little sister Rebecca. He kept wondering how she was doing. He could not remember her face, how she looked, and found himself thinking that she must look a lot like Lottie.

Billy seemed to prefer sitting backward on the mule, sucking his thumb. The only time he changed was when Francis gave them each a piece of the venison jerky he'd brought from the deer he'd killed. Billy grabbed the meat like a puppy—revealing a thumb that was amazingly white and clean—and almost swallowed it whole before going back to thumb sucking.

The silences were punctuated at intervals by Lottie, who would "go off," as Francis came to think of it, at the slightest provocation, the sunbonnet wobbling as she talked.

"See that buzzard up there? How can they fly like that without ever moving their wings, just hang there like they was floating on the air? Is it like they float there, like sticks float on water? How can the air be thick enough for them to float that way when it's still thin enough to breathe? I wish I could do that, just float up there and see it all forever and ever . . ."

The talk had a lulling effect and between the

boredom of the prairie—which he knew was deceptive—and Lottie going on, he soon fell into a kind of haze.

He should have known better. Every time he'd let his guard down something had come at him. But he rode and dozed, the mule following easily, and Lottie was talking about the neighbor Nancy.

". . . she goes to making things that are so pretty they take your breath away. Things to put on shelves and just look at, little boxes with trees on them and designs and colors—Oh."

The stopping startled Francis. His eyes had been half closed, his body rolling with the motion of the mare, his mind on a million other things and when she stopped talking he snapped his eyes open, but it was too late.

In front of him on either side were two Indian men. One had a rifle and the other a bow with an arrow in the string and they were both on foot—almost unheard of on the prairie. The one on the left was older, a grown man, the one on the right was young—fifteen, sixteen—and they were standing looking at him.

Francis's rifle was across his lap. The handgun hung in the sack off the saddle horn. The two extra rifles were back on the mule.

All of this, the Indians, the way they looked not twenty feet away, their weapons, his own weapons not being ready—all of this he registered in half a second. And at the same time he knew that there was no time. Even if he could swing the rifle up and get a shot off at one of them the other would get him.

It could have gone in any direction and for a full five seconds—it seemed like an hour—the tension was wound so tight Francis could hear his heart beating. He stared at them, they looked at him.

Then two things. He saw they were not wearing paint, which they would be wearing if they were looking to war, and at the same time the older of the two smiled and said something to the other who smiled as well.

They were looking back at Lottie and Billy— who was still sitting the mule backward, ignoring the Indians. Lottie had seen them but she had to hold her head back to peer out from beneath the flopping rim of her sunbonnet.

"Are they savages?" she asked.

"Be quiet," Francis said.

"Because if they are, you know, savages, then I think maybe you should do something. Of course I never have seen no savages and only heard about them in the wagon train where everybody said if they come upon you they'd cut you open and eat your heart and I don't want nobody cutting me open and eating my heart out so maybe . . ."

The older Indian's smile widened and he made a sign in front of his mouth, his fingers fluttering and moving away. Francis knew some sign from when he'd lived with the Indians, and literally the sign meant butterflies or birds flying. But in front of his mouth it meant words flying, and Francis nodded and smiled back and imitated the sign in front of his own mouth.

The young Indian put his bow down, took his fingers off the string and Francis knew it was over.

"English?" Francis asked, using sign. "Do you talk English?"

The boy shook his head, but the man nodded.

"Speak small, not big. Why you here?" His hands moved when he spoke, making sign to back up his spotty English.

"I'm looking for a wagon train. I've been lost." Francis also made sign, but he was not as good as the Indian and much slower.

"Young lost, too?"

Francis nodded. "I found them back almost a day. Their father died of the water sickness and I brought them with me."

Both of the Indians stepped back at this. They knew of cholera—Francis had heard of whole villages being killed in two or three days—and like Francis, they did not know how it spread.

"It's all right now," Francis said. "Good, good. They're not sick now. But that way a day"—he pointed in the direction they'd come—"that way there is a wagon where the sickness came from."

The man nodded and made a sign for peace—his palm up and facing out—and the boy did the same and Francis raised his hand and showed his palm.

"Hunt," the man said, pointing south, "that way."

Francis nodded and pointed west. "We go there." And because he couldn't resist it—the thought had been on his mind since he'd first seen them—he asked: "Why no horses?"

From living with and watching the Indians he knew they wouldn't move fifteen feet without a horse under them. They were all—man, woman, and child—better riders than Francis, and Jason Grimes had told him he thought they were born on a horse. Two men hunting on foot was rare.

But the man made the sign on his head for antlers. "Deer, better on foot, low, in grass. Closer. Shoot more. Horses back there with family." He made the sign for children and women. "Waiting for meat." He smiled.

Francis nodded, remembering the buck he'd killed by waiting in the grass. He started to say more but the mare moved under him, making him look down and when he looked up they were gone, vanished in the grass.

"I guess they weren't savages," Lottie said.

"No." Francis squeezed the mare with his legs and she started forward, the mule keeping up. "They were people, just like us, looking for food . . ."

The thought seemed to quiet Lottie, and Francis set the direction back to north and west but determined not to lose his alertness again.

The children posed a real problem. Alone, if something bad *did* happen he could cut and run and have a chance of getting out of it. There were horses faster than the mare, but not many quicker or more sure of foot, and that gave Francis some advantage.

But Lottie and Billy changed everything. The mule couldn't move fast, wouldn't carry them out of danger if it came, and that made it doubly important for Francis to be aware of what was coming to get time to react or hide.

Then there was food. He could go two, three days without eating but he didn't think it was good for young to go that long. They had to eat on a more regular basis. All he had left was the semi-dried venison and they ate from that most of the day, riding along—both children had been nearly starved and ate ravenously to make up for it—and the jerky was nearly gone.

He would have to hunt soon, get another deer or better yet a buffalo, which would slow them down, and at first that irritated him until he remembered that there wasn't a hurry to get anywhere because he didn't know where he was or where to go.

The problem was that suddenly the prairie was bare. Where he'd been seeing small groups of buffalo out ahead there didn't seem to be any for miles and he couldn't see deer or antelope.

They rode the rest of the day, Francis alert and looking for game and finally just before dusk he shot a jackrabbit.

"We'll stop for the night now," he said, lifting the children off the mule. "Gather wood for a fire so we can cook this rabbit . . ."

Lottie stretched and helped Billy take a few steps to shake his legs out. "Pa he tried to cook one of them once when we were with the wagon train and we like to broke our teeth chewing. We need some good meat, some more deer meat, that's the kind of meat we need. Some good red meat with fat on it to make drippings . . ."

She talked constantly, but she worked as she spoke, finding dry wood and sticks, and Billy helped her, and by the time Francis had finished hobbling the mare—the mule would stay without it—they had a stack of wood large enough to last all night.

Francis took some kindling sticks, shaved them with his knife to get curls, laid a fire and lit it.

"You keep wood on it," he told Lottie. "I'll clean the rabbit . . ."

He quickly gutted and skinned the rabbit and cut it into smaller pieces. There was no water where they stopped so he poured some from a canteen into the Dutch oven and put the rabbit into the water. He added a handful of flour for thickening and cut three chunks of venison to drop in on top. Then he put the lid on and shoved the cast pot into the fire.

"Stew," he said. "An hour or so . . ."

"I like stew," Lottie said. "I didn't mean back then that I didn't like stew and such like. I'm not a picky eater like some, being as I'll eat almost anything though I'm not fond of bugs nor the reptile along the ground. Billy here will eat a bug in a second. He just loves 'em. Not me, though . . ."

Billy was sitting on a blanket staring at the flames and Francis studied him. "Doesn't he ever talk?"

Lottie nodded. "Sure. He just don't have anything to say. Sometimes he'll talk your ear off. I remember once, I think it was last week, he looked me right in the eye and said 'I'm thirsty,' plain as day, must have been six, seven days ago . . ." She trailed off and the quiet was so sudden Francis thought she must have seen something. But he looked at her and saw she was crying quietly looking into the flames. "It was to Pa he said it. I miss Pa . . ."

Francis tried to think of something to say but there was nothing. He remembered when he'd first been kidnapped and then seen a toy that had belonged to his sister Rebecca and thought Rebecca was dead. The empty feeling. The numbness. No words could help.

So he put more wood on the fire and covered the two children to get them to sleep, and when they were at last both sleeping, he moved away from the fire to doze back in the grass with his rifle across his lap and a blanket over his shoulders. Twice in the night he heard wolves—they sang deeper and longer than the yipping coyotes—and he tried not to think of the children's father alone on the prairie.

Chapter Eleven

Lottie awakened early. Francis heard her as she broke small sticks and found red coals to blow on to make morning fire. They had all slept through the night without eating, and Francis decided it might have been the best thing possible for the meat stew he had prepared. It had cooked until the fire was out and when he came in by the fire Lottie had pulled the pot over to the flames and warmed it. Francis lifted the lid and the meat had become tender and fallen away from the bones.

He let the two children eat—Lottie was quiet

and he thought it was because she wasn't fully awake yet—and then finished what they did not want.

All of it didn't take an hour and it was just getting light in the east when they packed the bedrolls and loaded the mare and mule for the day. Francis helped them up on the mule—smiling as Billy turned around to sit backward—and mounted the mare and rode away from camp.

The day went smoothly. Clouds held to the horizon and then vanished and the sun was hot and welcome. A small breeze kept the flies down, and Francis figured Lottie's talker must have played out because other than ask a question now and then she was mostly quiet.

They quickly settled into the routine of riding, covering ground. Francis had turned straight west—had given up on hitting tracks—but in the middle of the afternoon they came to a ridge that was impossible to climb that stretched far away to the south and they had to turn north.

Fifteen or so miles north Francis could see the end of the ridge, and as they moved slowly in that direction, he could see dust near the end of the ridge. Lottie saw it as well and told him about it.

"Dust up there, you see it? Reminds me of the time when we were crossing that river just after we started before Pa he got the sickness. All the wagons had to wait in the same place so they corralled the stock until everybody was ready to ford the river and they raised *such* a cloud of dust . . ."

"It's buffalo," Francis said, squinting. "I can see them . . ."

But he was wrong.

Lottie was right, or partially so. As they moved closer—at a crawl, or so it felt to Francis—he could see the dust wasn't from buffalo but from moving wagons. It was a full train. But they weren't fording a river. When they were a mile off he counted twelve wagons, and they were bunched at the bottom of a steep upgrade with the horses and oxen corralled in a rope enclosure. The stock milling around was making the dust.

Whoever the train was made up of, he could travel with them. And somebody would take in the children.

They were nearly a quarter of a mile from the wagons—Francis could see individuals and hear the cracks of their whips as they worked the stock —when somebody from the wagon train noticed him.

There was a sudden movement that Francis thought looked like ants scurrying when an anthill has been kicked, and four men came running from the wagons to meet him.

They were all carrying rifles and they stopped

when Francis was still a hundred and fifty yards away, stopped and stood four abreast with their rifles across their chests.

They probably think we're Indians, Francis thought. Probably a mistake.

"I know those men," Lottie said suddenly in back of him.

"What?" He turned and the mare kept walking.

"That's the wagon train that drove us out when the sickness came. I know those four men. That's Peterson and Ellville and Johnson and McIntire and they were the ones to push us away and make us be where you found us and saved us . . ."

Francis turned back to the front. Pushing the sick ones out wasn't maybe nice, but it was the only thing they could do to save the rest. He understood that. But the sickness was past. Surely they wouldn't cause problems now.

When they were fifty yards away, the men leaned in together and spoke quickly amongst themselves, then faced Francis again.

"You can't come in to the wagons," the man on the left said. "Those children might be infected. We had to send them out."

Francis stopped the mare. Twenty-five yards. The one who spoke actually moved his rifle so the barrel was on Francis, and he thought, This is crazy. I'm not trying to hurt them. "They're all right now. It was their Pa who . . . took sick. These two are fine. And so am I."

"Just the same, we can't take the chance. We'll set some food and water out here for you and you turn and head out on your own." The man spoke to one of the others, who trotted back to the wagons and came back in a moment with a bucket of water and a loaf of bread.

All this time Francis sat holding the mare and the mule back. They had seen the stock and thought it was where they would spend the night and were anxious to end the day's ride.

He couldn't believe what he was hearing.

"I'm not . . . geared . . . for children. They need to be with wagons, people . . ."

The man shook his head. "I'm sorry but we can't. We have other children to think of and if they have the sickness and bring it back in . . . I'm taking a risk just standing here talking to you. It might blow on me and I could carry it back to the wagons."

"That's the same trash they talked when they sent us off before," Lottie said suddenly. "Just the same when Pa tried to get them to take us in and let him go off alone to be sick. They wouldn't do it then and they're talking the same trash now. You're just dirt, Frank McIntire. Just pig dirt and you know it."

Francis held his hand up to quiet Lottie and tried one more time. "I can go off alone—in fact I'd rather. I don't want to be with your train." Or, he thought, with any other train if they're all like this. "But these two are too young . . ."

"Just the same." McIntire stopped him. "We can't let you in. Ride on around if you like and pick up the trail, stay a quarter mile out, and God-speed to you. There's a trading post three days west by wagon. Maybe you can find help there, though I doubt it. When they find you're carrying the sickness, they won't let you come in."

"And if we push it?"

The man raised his rifle, as did the others. "We'll do what we have to do."

"Shoot us?"

"We'll do what we have to do," he repeated. "And be sorry for it later."

It was hopeless. Francis turned the mare to the side and began the long circle out around the train and back to the trail, the mule plodding behind.

He did not take the food and did not take the water and thought if he lived to be a hundred he would never take anything from people—good or bad—again.

Chapter Twelve

It wasn't much of a trading post. In fact it wasn't much of anything.

They rode a full day in what looked to be permanent ruts. After they rode around the wagon train—and the armed men followed them all around to make certain they kept going—Francis led the mule up the grade the wagons were trying to climb.

It was too steep for a wagon and they were using two-hundred-foot ropes and a triple team of horses on top to pull the wagons up one at a time.

But the grade didn't bother the mare or the mule at all and when they came out on top where there was a stony ledge Francis was amazed to see that the trail was so used it cut into the stone itself.

Grooves left the top of the ridge and headed west into the prairie, grooves a foot deep in the hard sod, and the grass was eaten down so much along the way that the ground had turned to dust. It almost made Francis smile—he'd been worried about losing the trail. He couldn't have lost this if he were blind.

It was absolutely flat. Even the small rolling hills seemed to have flattened out and the three days it would have taken a wagon to get to the post were only a day and a half on the mare and mule.

They stopped for the night in a dry, fireless camp. There were no springs, and preceding wagons and people had burned every available stick of dry wood or even dry buffalo manure so they couldn't build a fire. There was also no grass for the animals anywhere near the trail. Stock from wagon trains had eaten it down so low that even the roots were gone and the earth was a dry, empty powder.

Francis almost smiled that night, again thinking of his worry about finding the trail. Camp was a miserable affair, dark and with no fire to cheer them. They ate the last of the venison jerky—both Lottie and Billy sneezing from the dust that seemed to fill the air, even at night—and Francis slept fitfully because there was no way to conceal himself in case trouble came. It was like trying to sleep on top of an immense, dusty table.

They were out of everything but water and flour in the morning so they drank water and each took a mouthful of raw flour, and they started before sunup, the dust coming up from the hooves, clogging their nose and eyes.

Francis tried swinging away from the main part of the trail but many had already done it, thousands—Jason Grimes had said they were coming from the East so thick it was like swarming bees—and the dust was everywhere so he wrapped pieces cut from the tarp around Lottie and Billy and just kept slogging.

The "trading post" came as a complete surprise. A small breeze had come up, making the dust worse, and Francis had been looking down to keep his eyes from filling when suddenly the mare stopped.

He nudged her without looking up, but she didn't go and when he looked up he saw it was because she had her shoulders against the top rail of a fence. Actually it was less a fence than a crude collection of broken wagon parts—tongues, boards from the sides, old wheels, all lashed together to make a ramshackle corral. To the right was a gate made from the large rear wheel of a wagon and over the gate a rough sign lettered in what looked like charcoal said:

STOCK BOARDED
TWENNY SENTS THE NITE

Francis doubted that the board included anything like feed or grass in this stripped land.

He raised his eyes and squinted and through gusts in the blowing dirt he saw a series of small shacks arranged on the other side of the corral. Like the boarding pen they were made from old wagon parts gleaned from wreckage on the trail. It looked more like a junkyard for old wagons than anything else.

And it also looked deserted. He peered inside the huts as best he could but couldn't see anything for a full minute and a half.

Then a tarp curtain over one of the openings—it couldn't be called a door—was pushed back, and a face showed for a moment, then disappeared and reappeared a moment later with a hat on.

A thin man, tall and sunken, with a dark beard trimmed short and pointed on the end came out of the hut and approached Francis. He put one hand on the mare's bridle, and she pulled her head away and wiggled her ears, a sign of nervousness.

"You'll be wanting to board the animals?" He spoke in a low voice, almost a hiss, and Francis suddenly thought of snakes and Courtweiler in that order.

Near the huts the wind had died and Francis could see better. He shook his head. "I don't have any money. But I need a home for the young ones. I found them in a deserted wagon on the prairie—I think their father was killed by a bear." (A white lie can't hurt, he thought.) "Is there room for them here?"

"Cholera, you mean." The man smiled shrewdly and inspected Lottie and Billy more closely. "Don't make no never mind to me. I've had it and so's my missus. Onct you've had it you cain't take it again." He pushed the tarp back and looked at Billy and Lottie more closely, pinched their arms. "They don't look sickly. 'Pears they could pull their own weight, anyways. Good, I'll take 'em."

He lifted them off the mule and carried them into the hut without another word and Francis sat feeling uncomfortable. On the one hand he wanted a home for them, but the man was . . . was so wrong somehow.

He shrugged the feeling off and dismounted. They would have a better chance here and maybe a train would come along after the one that shunned them that wouldn't mind taking them on. They would be better off, he thought again, but he tied the mare to the corral fence and made his way to the hut to lift the tarp sideways and peer inside.

The man was in there, doing something with a bucket and a water barrel, his back to the opening. There was also a woman, the man's wife, and she was as thin as the man, had the same angular look about her, a sunken hungry look. But she had Billy in her lap and was pinching Lottie's cheek and smiling, and Francis dropped the tarp back and returned to the horse.

It would be all right. They'd be safer here than trying to ride with Francis.

The man came out of the hut with a bucket of water. "Your stock will need water," he said.

"Thank you."

"It's four cents the bucket," he said quickly. "You got four cents?"

Francis stared at the man. Four cents for a bucket of water? Then he shook his head. "No. I don't have any money."

"You got something to trade?"

"For four cents?"

"For the water."

"I need some supplies and I've got two rifles to trade." He thought suddenly of the pistol and added, "I've got a pistol as well, but it belongs to the children."

"I'll take it for 'em," he said. "And you know, keep it. For them. What supplies you need?"

"Flour and sugar and some bacon . . ."

"How many rifles did you say?"

"Two."

"You don't know the prices here, do you?"

"No."

"A rifle will bring you flour, or sugar, or bacon. Not all of them, just one of them. Ten pounds of flour, five pounds of sugar, five pounds of bacon."

"For a *rifle*?"

"Ayup. Which do you want?"

Francis shook his head. It was robbery but he had no need for Dubs's rifle and he did need flour. "Flour. One rifle's worth. And you throw in that bucket of water for the mare and mule."

"Would you be looking for getting shed of that mule? It seems about to die on you."

Francis looked at the mule and thought how much better it looked now than it had when he first saw it and smiled. "That mule will still be going when you're done, mister. He stays with me."

"Just as you say."

"I could work for you," Francis said. "To pay off other supplies."

"Don't need it now."

"Well then, that's it."

The man went back into one of the huts while

Francis watered the mule and mare, and he came out in a couple of minutes carrying a cloth feed sack with ten pounds of flour and handed it to Francis to tie on his saddle.

Francis handed him Dubs's rifle and mounted the mare and took the lead rope from the mule and rode off into the dust without looking back, forcing himself to not look back.

Chapter Thirteen

He made it nearly ten miles. The wind stopped and the dust abated somewhat and he kept riding until just before dark. He had angled north, still following the trail but looking for grass and water, and when he was some five or six miles north of the trail, he started to find grass for the animals, and just before dark he hit a spring.

There was wood for a fire, and he shot a rabbit on the way in to the spring and made stew and sat by the fire and was miserable.

Jason Grimes came back to him, the memory of

the man, his rough humor and final viciousness. It seemed years ago yet it wasn't a month since the fight with Braid, and Francis had changed almost daily.

He was nothing like the boy who had started West and he thought of that, was dismayed to realize he couldn't remember how his mother and father looked, how his sister Rebecca sounded. They'd had a dog, a little feisty dog, and he couldn't remember how the dog looked.

Lottie and Billy were there suddenly, cutting into his thoughts. He lay back and looked at the stars—they seemed to be all around him, somehow under him as well as over—and he thought of Lottie with her sunbonnet flopping down all the time and Billy sitting backward on the mule and they were more real to him than Jason Grimes or even his family.

And something the man had said. What was it? Something he had said about Francis working to pay for trade goods. Francis sat up, trying to remember, but it didn't come and he finally could fight the exhaustion no longer.

He put more wood on the fire and took his bedroll and moved back in the grass with his rifle to where a small hummock provided cover and settled in for the night. I am fourteen, he thought, no, wait, maybe I'm fifteen. I'm fifteen and I sleep on the ground with a rifle and I am alone in the world and I am ready to rest . . .

But sleep wouldn't come, didn't come, and by the time the eastern sky started to gather light he was already saddled and moving.

If I keep going, he thought, and get farther away, if I just keep going it will go away, this feeling. But it didn't. The uneasiness grew until it became real, something in back of him, and he actually turned twice to see the mule plodding along expecting, fully expecting to see Lottie riding and Billy sitting backward.

But of course they were not there and he went another mile, riding more and more slowly and finally without meaning to his hand pulled back on the mare's rein and she stopped and he sat. Thinking.

Then it hit him. What the man had said. He'd said he didn't need any help *now*. It was a strange way to put it and Francis remembered how he had pinched the children's arms, how the woman felt them as well.

They were going to work the kids, just use them. Like stock. He was sure of it.

He turned the mare. It was wrong, leaving them. Francis should have found them a good family or should have stayed to protect them.

Should protect them now.

He kicked the mare in the ribs and took her up to a distance-covering trot. He had come slowly after leaving the post and if he kept her moving they should get back in three or four hours.

He'd just make sure the children were all right and then he could turn around and come away again. And if they weren't . . . well, he'd cover that when he got there. He was probably wrong. They were probably fine and it was all in his head.

But soon the mare was moving faster, into a canter and the mule thundered to keep up.

When he was still four or five miles from the post he could see that it had all changed. The wagon train that had forced them to stay out had come to the post and were pulled up to camp nearby. There was no wind, but the stock had churned the ground and clouds of dust floated in the air obscuring the people.

As he rode closer he could see that the wagon train was keeping well away from the compound. They must have found out that Lottie and Billy were here, he thought, and they're scared of taking the sickness. He smiled.

Then he rounded a corner near the corral and saw Lottie and Billy, and the smile died. They were each carrying two buckets of water—in Billy's case the buckets looked as big as he was and he dragged more than carried them—and they were both crying. Even in the endless dust he could see streaks down their cheeks, and when Lottie saw Francis she dropped her buckets and ran toward him.

Francis swung off the mare and she hit him about when he hit the ground. Billy had done the same—both his buckets spilled—but he stopped about three feet away and turned his back.

Lottie moved back and pushed her bonnet up. "It's right good to see you. Time was I never thought it would be good to see someone again, except Pa, of course, and Ma, but then you went and left us here . . ."

"What's the matter? Why were you crying?"

Lottie shook her head. "No reason. Just happy to see you . . ."

"He beat us." Billy spoke with his back to Francis. "He took a cane rod and he beat Lottie and when I tried to stop him he beat me."

"Beat you? Why?"

"For not working hard enough," Lottie answered. "I wasn't moving buckets of water fast enough out to where the train people could get them for the stock and like Billy said he took a cane to me. But it wasn't much. Like a bee sting . . ."

She stopped talking because Francis had picked her up and put her on the mule. Then he reached for Billy and had him halfway up when a voice stopped him.

"What you doing with them children?"

Francis finished setting Billy on the mule—backward—and turned. The trading-post owner was there, twenty feet away. His wife had come out of one of the huts as well and stood with one hand on the doorway, staring at him.

"I'm taking them."

"No, you ain't. Them are my kids now and I'll keep 'em. You gave 'em to me fair and square and I've got an *in*vestment in them. I'll be taking them back now. They got to work off their 'debtedness. It's the law."

Francis was by the mare and he stopped with one hand on the saddle horn, his rifle in the other, half turned toward the man. "You touch them, either one, one more time and you'll pull back a bloody stump."

"Oh, you're tough, are you? Just a regular bobcat."

And it all swirled through Francis then. Captured by the Indians, beaten, escaping, living with Jason Grimes, trapping, blizzards—all in a sudden flash it went through him. All that, and he was still alive and had both arms and legs and he smiled. "Why, yes, I believe I am."

He swung up on the mare and caught up the mule's catch rope and they rode away silently and they were a good two miles away from the trading post, angling north to find the grass and water so they could camp, just over two miles when it hit Francis.

"Billy talked," he said to Lottie. "Back there he talked just fine."

Lottie nodded. "It was the first time he felt like he had something to say. I told you he could talk, but you don't listen to me. Just like I told you it was wrong to leave us with that awful man . . ."

"You didn't tell me."

"Yes, I did. Or I meant to and it's the same thing. I meant to tell you and you should have known it. But it doesn't matter now 'cause we're back together and the whole thing reminds me of the time our neighbor lady, Nancy, lost all her chickens and thought it was a wolf come to her coop but it wasn't, it was one of the Mayfield boys took 'em as a joke except when Nancy found out she put a load of rock salt in his butt with a shotgun and he didn't laugh so much. She was something, Nancy. I recollect the time she made biscuits and didn't get the shortening right and they were so heavy they would sink in water . . ."

Francis steered the mare with his knees, his rifle across his lap, and smiled, letting the words wash over him. Away from the trading post there was no dust, the afternoon sun was warm on his back, and the weather looked to stay good for some time. He had no plans other than to keep moving west and no hurry to get anywhere. He'd take meat later—maybe a buffalo—and they could stock up.

It was all in all, he thought, his smile widening, a good day to take his family for a ride, maybe go see the country.

A very good day.

**DON'T MISS ANY OF THE BOOKS IN
THE TUCKET ADVENTURES!**

THE ADVENTURES BEGIN . . .

Fourteen-year-old Francis Tucket is heading west on
the Oregon Trail with his family by wagon train.
When he receives a rifle for his birthday, he is thrilled
that he is being treated like an adult. But Francis lags
behind to practice shooting and is captured by
Pawnees. It will take wild horses, hostile tribes, and a
mysterious one-armed mountain man named Mr.
Grimes to help Francis become the man who will be
called Mr. Tucket.

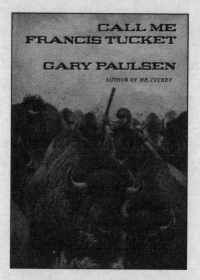

Alone. Francis Tucket now feels more confident that he can handle almost anything. A year ago, on the wagon train, he was kidnapped from his family by a Pawnee hunting party. Then he escaped with the help of the mountain man Mr. Grimes. Now that he and Mr. Grimes have parted ways, Francis is heading west on his Indian pony, crossing the endless prairie, trying to find his family. After a year with Mr. Grimes, Francis has learned to live by the harsh code of the wilderness. He can cause a stampede, survive his own mistakes, and face up to desperadoes. But when he rescues a little girl and her younger brother, Francis takes on more than he bargained for.

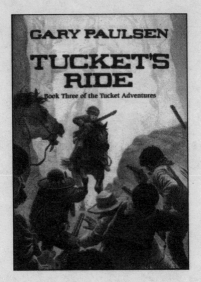

Francis Tucket and his adopted family, Lottie and Billy, are heading west in search of Francis's parents on the Oregon Trail. But when winter comes early, Francis turns south to avoid the cold and leads them right into enemy territory. The United States and Mexico are at war, and Francis, Lottie, and Billy are captured by the most ruthless band of outlaws Francis has ever seen. The outlaws are taking them away— away from the trail west, away from civilization, and away from any chance of rescue.

GARY PAULSEN

TUCKET'S GOLD

Book Four of the Tucket Adventures

Things look grim for fifteen-year-old Francis Tucket and his adopted family, young Lottie and Billy. Without horses, water, or food, they're alone in a prairie wasteland, with the dreaded Comanchero outlaws in pursuit. Enemies old and new wait at every turn, and death might strike at any moment. But so might good fortune. The three stumble upon an ancient treasure and use teamwork, courage, and fast thinking to hold on to it. When they discover a hidden village, the West doesn't seem so wild after all.

FRANCIS HEADS HOME AT LAST. . . .

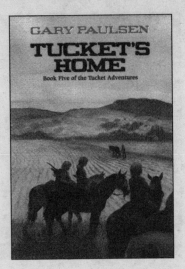

Francis Tucket and his adopted family, Billy and Lottie, have survived hair-raising and rip-roaring adventures as they have struggled west, held together by their goal to find Francis's family on the Oregon Trail. They also share a secret: the treasure hidden in their saddlebags. Now the three meet up with a British adventurer, with men of faith and hope, and with bloodthirsty ex-soldiers. Even here, at the end of the trail, surprises and tragic turns await them.